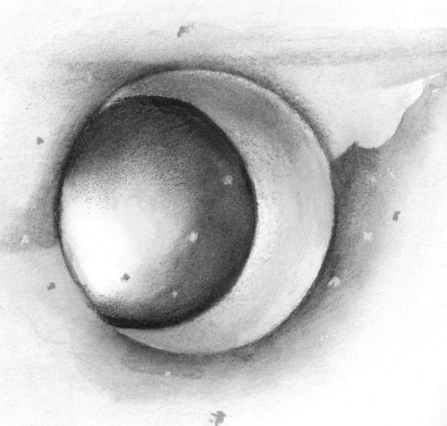

Night on Neighborhood Street

by Eloise Greenfield

pictures by Jan Spivey Gilchrist

SCHOLASTIC INC.

New York Toronto London Auckland Sydney
Mexico City New Delhi Hong Kong

I acknowledge, with gratitude, the support of the
National Endowment for the Arts in Washington, D.C.,
a federal agency; and the D.C. Commission on the
Arts and Humanities.   —E.G.

ISBN 0-439-28349-3

To Marie Dutton Brown
for her steadfast commitment
to spread the true story
of African American people
—E.G.

In loving memory of
my "Mama" Arthric Spivey
who lived her life on Neighborhood Street
—J.S.G.

Neighborhood Street

The street had stretched awake
as dawn spun slowly
out of darkness
morning mamas and daddies
roused the children
with soft sugar-names
and the scent of hot buttered
bread
now the day has sped 'round
to evening
and children ring the sidewalk
singing
Ohhh, li'l Liza
li'l Liza Jane
dusk spins from daylight
and the children sing
We're goin' around the mountain
two by two
circling the mountain
as night falls
Rise, Sally, rise
on Neighborhood Street

Little Boy Blues

He's got the little boy blues
He's all alone
Waiting for his best, best
Friend to come home
Looking at the moon
With a sad, sad eye
Poking out his mouth
Getting ready to cry
Going to sit right there
Until Saturday night
When his friend gets home
Going to hold him tight
Got more lonesome
Than he can use
He's got the bad, bad
Long face, hurtin'
Little boy blues

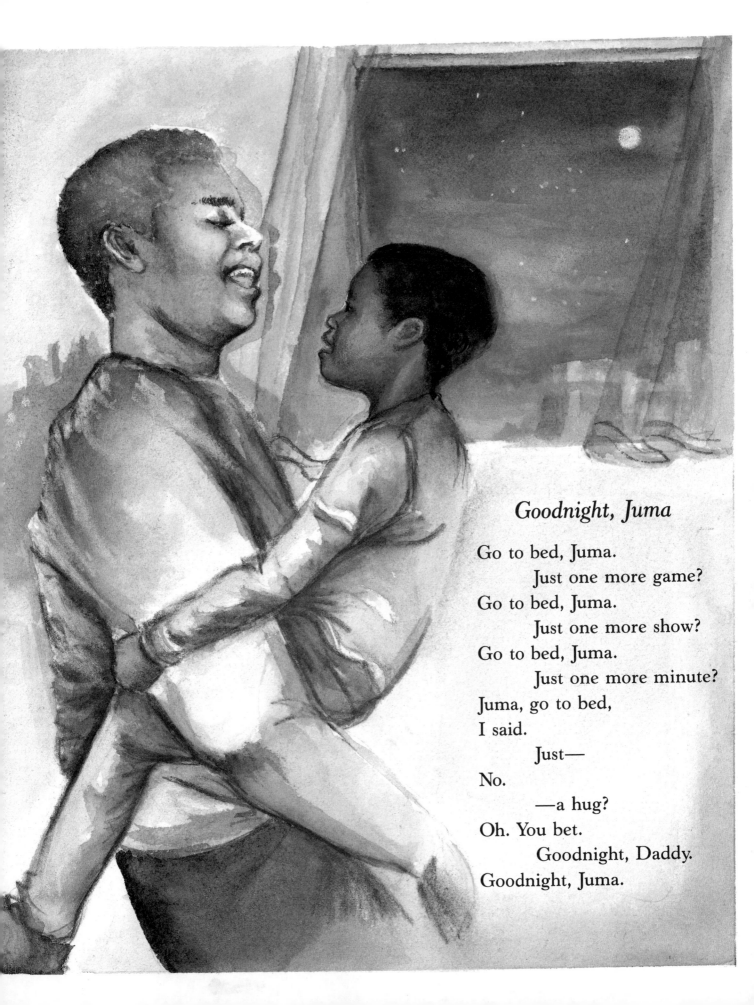

Goodnight, Juma

Go to bed, Juma.
      Just one more game?
Go to bed, Juma.
      Just one more show?
Go to bed, Juma.
      Just one more minute?
Juma, go to bed,
I said.
      Just—
No.
      —a hug?
Oh. You bet.
      Goodnight, Daddy.
Goodnight, Juma.

New Baby Poem (1)

all day she has slept
now is her time
to cry
"Where am I?
I'm too tiny a girl
for this big new world."

New Baby Poem (II)

sleep coming down
bringing dreams that
swish
like the sound of
warm water
rocking the baby
rocking the baby
swish, swish
swish

The Seller

when the seller comes around
carrying in his many pockets
packages of death
all the children go inside
they see behind his easy smile
they know his breath is cold
they turn their backs and
reach for warmth
and life

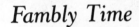

Fambly Time

When the Robinsons gather
Just before bed
The kids in pajamas
The homework's been read
It's time for the family
To have some fun
"It's fambly time!"
Says the littlest one

They come from work
They come from play
They get together
At the end of the day
For singing and guessing
And games of rhyme
For jokes and jacks
And pantomime
And the little one calls it
"Fambly time!"

The Meeting

some nights they meet—
the people who live on
Neighborhood Street
get together to talk things out
work things out
and there's this brother who
always tries to pick a fight
says he's the only one who's right
his face gets ugly and he
starts to shout
he don't know what he's talking about
everybody just leans back and waits
and nods and smiles and says
"unh hunh, unh hunh" until
he sees that what they mean
is there's the door
and then he don't say
no more

When Tonya's Friends Come to Spend the Night

When Tonya's friends come to spend the night
Her mama's more than just polite
She says she's glad they came to call
Tells them that she loves them all
Listens to what they can do
Tells them what she's good at, too
Plays her horn and lets them sing
(Do they make that music swing!)
Feeds them sweet banana bread
Hugs them when it's time for bed
Tonya sure would have a gripe
If she were the jealous type
But she isn't just a guest
She knows her mama loves her best

The House
With the Wooden Windows

The house with the wooden windows
doesn't know night from day
doesn't know its neighbors
or the tales the children tell
to scare the babies
They say the house is filled with ghosts
that boogie when the moon is right
but the house is empty
and knows that only dust rises
to dance to the lonely beat
of silence

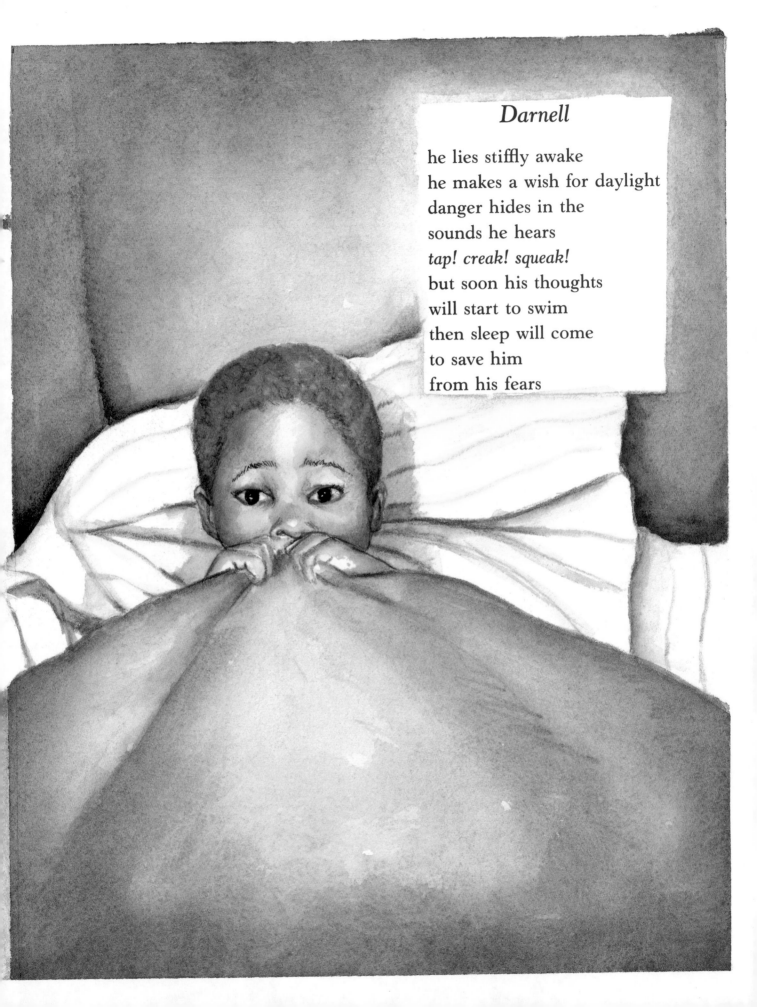

Darnell

he lies stiffly awake
he makes a wish for daylight
danger hides in the
sounds he hears
tap! creak! squeak!
but soon his thoughts
will start to swim
then sleep will come
to save him
from his fears

Buddy's Drea[m]

Not just one, but two of [him]
Side by side, limb by lim[b]
Arms do the wiggle, legs kick [...]
Moving to the music, he's a mighty pair
A crowd is there
Saying
Go, Buddy, Buddy
Go, Buddy, Go
Go, Buddy, Buddy
Go, Buddy, Go

Not just two, but four of him
Back to back, limb to limb
Dancing on the tables, whirling on the floor
Turning like a turbo, he's a terrible four
The people roar
Saying
Go, Buddy, Buddy
Go, Buddy, Go
Go, Buddy, Buddy
Go, Buddy, Go
He's going, going, going
He's gone!

In the Church

In the church
the congregation is
singing songs of praise
raising their swaying arms
to Glory
Hallelujah they sing
going to give up their sins
give up their pain
going to start a new life
shed their old ways
at the altar
In the church
the congregation is swaying
singing songs of praise
raising their arms
and their voices
to Glory

Nerissa

Her daddy's out of work
and her mama's sick in bed
Nerissa tries to think of things
to make them glad
she can't bring dinner
like the neighbors do
she can't mend the hole
in her daddy's shoe
but she's a big help
when she tickles her folks
by telling them the best old
bedtime jokes

Karen

Karen lets her
sister be the mama
evenings
when Mama's at work
mostly minds and
bedtimes doesn't fuss
much
just yawns wide, then waits
for her sister to tender
a mama's kiss

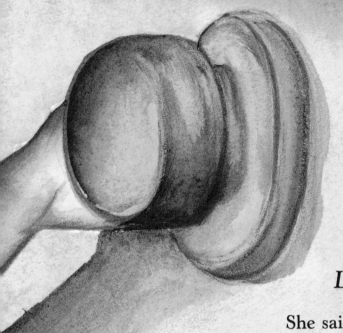

Lawanda's Walk

She said she wasn't sleepy
She said it extra loud
She didn't want to be carried
She wanted to be proud
She tried not to lean
Or let her eyelids droop
But the longest walk she ever took
Was the walk from car to stoop
She said she wasn't a baby
She tried to say it right
But the words all ran together
And spilled into the night
Then she leaned against her daddy
For help, but not before
She felt the knob and knew
That she had made it to the door
She closed her eyes but not before
She made it to the door

Night on Neighborhood Street

only light and shadow
play on the sidewalk now
it is the time when
darkness and stillness meet
and most are asleep
on Neighborhood Street
then Tonya's mama
out for a breath of air
blows lullaby sounds
into the silence
the children hear and smile
their sleep deepens
and they are at peace
with the night